LIMERICK LIBRARIES

3 0027 00806145 6

KU-190-365

WITHDRAWN FROM STOCK

Text and illustrations copyright
© Terry Fan and Eric Fan 2016 •
The right of Terry Fan and Eric
Fan to be identified as the author and
illustrator of this work has been asserted by
them in accordance with the Copyright, Designs
and Patents Act, 1988 (United Kingdom) • First
published in the United States by Simon & Schuster
Books for Young Readers, an imprint of Simon & Schuster
Children's Publishing Division, 1230 Avenue of the Americas,
New York, New York 10020 • First published in Great Britain in
2017 by Frances Lincoln Children's Books, 74–77 White Lion Street,
London N1 9PF • QuartoKnows.com • Visit our blogs at QuartoKnows.
com • All rights reserved. • No part of this publication may be reproduced,
stored in a retrieval system, or transmitted, in any form, or by any means, electrical,
mechanical, photocopying, recording or otherwise without the prior permission of
the publisher or a licence permitting restricted copying. In the United Kingdom such
licences are issued by the Copyright Licensing Agency, Barnard's Inn, 86 Fetter Lane,
London EC4A 1EN • A catalogue record for this book is available from the British Library •
ISBN 978-184780-939-1 • Original book design by Lizzy Bromley • The text for this book is set in Adobe
Garamond. • The illustrations for this book are rendered in graphite and coloured digitally. • Printed in China •
10 9 8 7 6 5 4 3 2

WITHDRAWN FROM STOCK

FOR MUM AND DAD
—T. F. & E. F.

The NIGHT GARDENER

Terry Fan & Eric Fan

WITHDRAWN FROM STOCK

Frances Lincoln
Children's Books

LIMERICK CITY AND COUNTY
LIBRARY
00806145

William looked out of his window
to find a commotion on the street.
He quickly dressed, ran downstairs
and raced out of the door to discover…

a wise owl had appeared overnight, as if by magic.
William spent the whole day staring at it in wonder,

and he continued to stare until it
became too dark to see.

That night he went to sleep
with a sense of excitement.

The following morning,

William was not disappointed.

Each day William discovered a new topiary.
Next was a friendly rabbit,

followed by a pretty parakeet...

and then a playful elephant.

With each new sculpture, the crowds grew and grew.

Something was happening on Grimloch Lane.

Something good.

The next day, William dashed out of his home

and followed the crowds, only to find...

the most magnificent masterpiece yet!

Festivities continued
long after the sun had set.

As William was about
to head home,

he spotted someone unfamiliar.

Could it be?

The gentleman turned to William.
"There are so many trees in this park
I could use a little help."
It *was* the Night Gardener!

LIMERICK CITY AND COUNTY LIBRARY

Under the light of
a full moon,

they worked deep
into the night.

William awoke to the sound of happy families walking by,

and a gift from the Night Gardener.

The whole town had come out to admire the
Night Gardener's – and William's – hard work.

Over time the leaves changed…

and then fell,

until there was no evidence
that the Night Gardener
had ever been to
Grimloch Lane.

But the people of the small town
were never the same.

And neither was William.

WITHDRAWN FROM STOCK